The Kitten Who Thought He Was A Mouse

The Kitten Who Thought He Was A Mouse

By Miriam Norton
Illustrated by Garth Williams

A GOLDEN BOOKS® PAPERBACK
Golden Books®
Western Publishing Company, Inc.
850 Third Avenue, New York, N.Y. 10022

There were five Miggses: Mother and Father Miggs and Lester and two sisters.

They had, as field mice usually do, an outdoor nest
for summer in an empty lot and an indoor nest for
winter in a nearby house.

They were very surprised one summer day to find
a strange bundle in their nest, a small gray and black
bundle of fur and ears and legs, with eyes not yet open.
They knew by its mewing that the bundle must be a
kitten, a lost kitten with no family and no name.

"Poor kitty," said the sisters.
"Let him stay with us," said Lester.
"But a *cat*!" said Mother Miggs.

"Why not?" said Father Miggs.

"We can bring him up to be a good mouse. He need never find out he is really a cat. You'll see—he'll be a good thing for this family."

"Let's call him Mickey," said Lester.

And that's how Mickey Miggs found his new family and a name.

After his eyes opened, he began to grow up just as mice do, eating all kinds of seeds and bugs and drinking from puddles and sleeping in a cozy pile of brother and sister mice.

Father Miggs showed him his first tomcat—at a safe distance— and warned him to "keep away from all cats and dogs and people."

Mickey saw his first mousetrap—"The most dangerous thing of all," said Mother Miggs—when they moved to the indoor nest that fall.

He was too clumsy to steal bait from traps himself, so Lester and the sisters had to share with him what they stole.

But Mickey was useful in fooling the household cat, Hazel. He practiced up on meowing, for usually, of course, he squeaked, and became clever at what he thought was imitating a cat.

He would hide in a dark corner and then, "Meow!
Meow!" he'd cry. Hazel would poke around, leaving the
pantry shelves unguarded while she looked for the other
cat. That gave Lester and his sisters a chance to make a
raid on the leftovers.

Poor Hazel! She knew she heard, even smelled,
another cat, and sometimes saw cat's eyes shining in a
corner. But no cat ever came out to meet her.

How could she know that Mickey didn't know he was a cat at all and that he feared Hazel as much as the mousiest mouse would!

And so Mickey Miggs grew, becoming a better mouse all the time and enjoying his life. He loved cheese, bacon, and cake crumbs. He got especially good at smelling out potato skins and led the sisters and Lester straight to them every time.

"A wholesome and uncatlike food," said Mother Miggs to Father Miggs approvingly. "Mickey is doing well." And Father Miggs said to Mother Miggs, "I told you so!"

Then one day, coming from a nap in the wastepaper basket, Mickey met the children of the house, Peggy and Paul.

"*Ee-eeeeek!*" Mickey squeaked in terror. He dashed along the walls of the room, looking for his mousehole.

"It's a kitten!" cried Peggy as Mickey squeezed through the hold.

"But it acts like a mouse," said Paul.

The children could not understand why the kitten had been so mouselike, but they decided to try to make friends with him.

That night, as Mickey came out of his hole, he nearly tripped over something lying right there in front of him. He sniffed at it. It was a dish and in the dish was something to drink.

"What is it?" asked Mickey. Lester didn't know, but timidly tried a little. "No good," he said, shaking his whiskers.

Mickey tried it, tried some more, then some more, and some more and more and more—until it was all gone.

"Mmmmm!" he said. "What wonderful stuff."

"It's probably poison and you'll get sick," said Lester disgustedly. But it wasn't poison and Mickey had a lovely feeling in his stomach from drinking it. It was milk, of course. And every night that week Mickey found a saucer of milk outside that same hole. He lapped up every drop.

"He drank it, he drank it!" cried Peggy and Paul happily each morning. They began to set out a saucerful in the daytime, too.

At first Mickey would drink the milk only when he was sure Peggy and Paul were nowhere around. Soon he grew bolder and began to trust them in the room with him.

And soon he began to let them come nearer and nearer and nearer still.

Then one day he found himself scooped up and held in Peggy's arms. He didn't feel scared. He felt fine. And he felt a queer noise rumble up his back and all through him. It was Mickey's first purr.

Peggy and Paul took Mickey to a shiny glass on the wall and held him close in front of it. Mickey, who had never seen a mirror, saw a cat staring at him there, a cat in Paul's hands, where he thought *he* was. He began to cry, and his cry, instead of being a squeak, was a mewing wail.

Finally Mickey began to understand that he was not
a mouse like Lester and his sisters, but a cat like Hazel.
He stayed with Peggy and Paul that night, trying not
to be afraid of his own cat-self. He still didn't quite
believe it all, however, and next morning he crept back
through his old hole straight to Mother Miggs.

"Am I really a cat?" he cried.

"Yes," said Mother Miggs sadly. And she told him the whole story of how he was adopted and brought up as a mouse. "We loved you and wanted you to love us," she explained. "It was the only safe and fair way to bring you up."

After talking with Mother Miggs, Mickey decided to be a cat in all ways. He now lives with Peggy and Paul, who also love him and who can give him lots of good milk and who aren't afraid of his purr or his meow.

Mickey can't really forget his upbringing, however. He takes an old rubber mouse of Peggy's to bed with him.

He often visits the Miggses in the indoor nest, where
he nibbles cheese tidbits and squeaks about old times.
And of course he sees to it that Hazel no longer
prowls in the pantry at night.

"Oh, I'm so fat and stuffed from eating so much in Hazel's pantry," Father Miggs often says happily to Mother Miggs. "I always said our Mickey would be a good thing for the family—and he is!"

Miriam Norton wrote *The Kitten Who Thought He Was A Mouse* in 1951.

Garth Williams has had a long and illustrious career as an illustrator of children's books, many of which are now considered classics, among them *Stuart Little* and *Charlotte's Web* by E. B. White and *The Cricket in Times Square* by George Selden. *The Kitten Who Thought He Was A Mouse* is only one of the many books Williams illustrated for Golden Books in the 1940s and 1950s.